HOW LOUD IS A LION?

Stella Blackstone & Clare Beaton

Parrots are feathery, porcupines are prickly,
But how loud is a lion? Shhh! Listen!

Giraffes are gentle, gazelles are graceful,
But how loud is a lion? Shhh! Listen!

Cheetahs are spotty, zebras are stripy,
But how loud is a lion? Shhh! Listen!

Hoopoes are happy, chimpanzees are cheeky,
But how loud is a lion? Shhh! Listen!

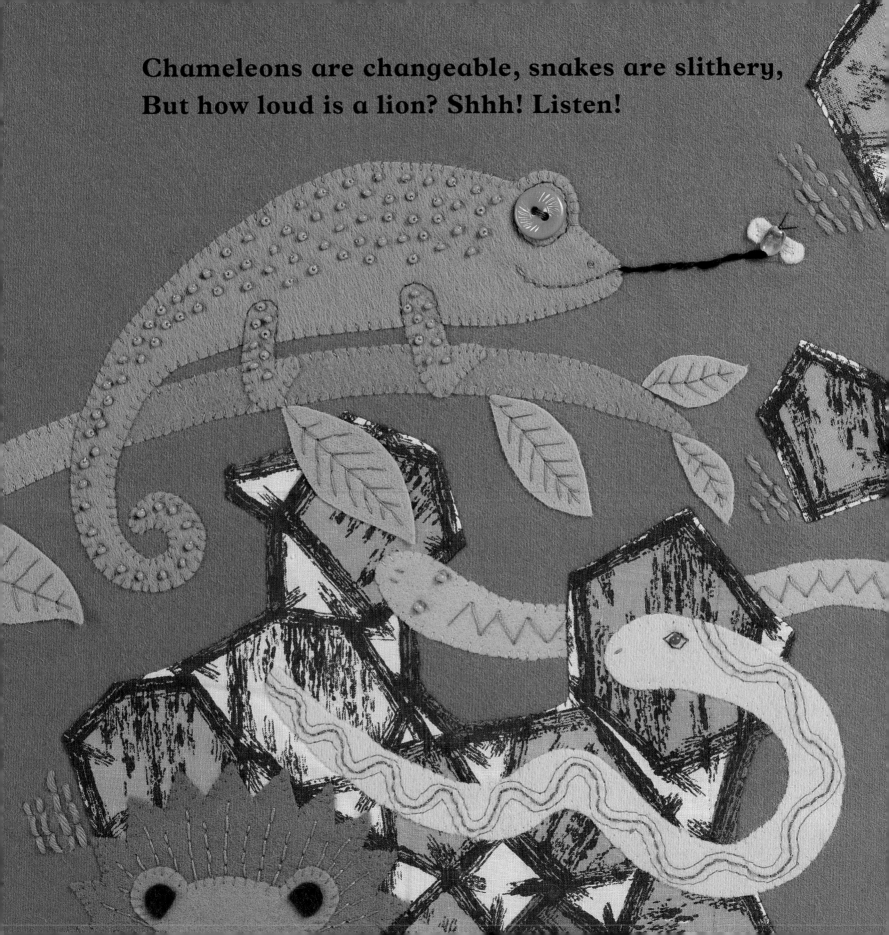

Chameleons are changeable, snakes are slithery,
But how loud is a lion? Shhh! Listen!

Antelopes are elegant, elephants are enormous,
But how loud is a lion? Shhh! Listen!

Crocodiles are crafty, monkeys are mischievous,
But how loud is a lion? Shhh! Listen!

Gorillas are grizzly, zorillas are greedy,
But how loud is a lion? Shhh! Listen!

Hippos are heavy, rhinos are hefty,
But how loud is a lion? Shhh! Listen!

Shhh!

For Francis — S. B.
For my daughter, Kate — C. B.

Barefoot Books
124 Walcot Street
Bath BA1 5BG

Barefoot Books
2067 Massachusetts Ave
Cambridge, MA 02140

Text copyright © 2002 by Stella Blackstone
Illustrations copyright © 2002 by Clare Beaton

The moral rights of Stella Blackstone and Clare Beaton have been asserted
First published in the United States of America by Barefoot Books, Inc.
and in Great Britain by Barefoot Books, Ltd in 2002
This paperback edition published in 2011
All rights reserved. Printed in China by Printplus, Ltd on 100% acid-free paper

Graphic design by Judy Linard, London
Reproduction by B & P International, Hong Kong

This book was typeset in Plantin Schoolbook Bold 20 on 28 point
The illustrations were prepared in felt with braid, beads and sequins

ISBN 978-1-84686-534-3

British Cataloguing-in-Publication Data: a catalogue record
for this book is available from the British Library

Library of Congress Cataloging-in-Publication
Data is available under LCCN 2005022104

1 3 5 7 9 8 6 4 2